Thanks to César, for putting such enthusiasm into this book

Thanks to Benjamin's parents and Manel for their help.

Thanks to my families—both the one I got and the one I chose.

Thanks to my readers.

Library of Congress Cataloging-in-Publication Data

Montserrat, Pep.
  Ms. Rubinstein's beauty / Pep Montserrat.
    p. cm.
  Summary: When Mr. Pavlov and Ms. Rubinstein look beyond one another's strange characteristics, they discover beauty and grace that no one else has ever noticed.
  ISBN-13: 978-1-4027-3063-4
  ISBN-10: 1-4027-3063-2
  [1. Beauty, Personal—Fiction. 2. Abnormalities, Human—Fiction. 3. Circus performers—Fiction. 4. Individuality—Fiction.] I. Title.

PZ7.M7713Ms 2006
[E]—dc22
                                2005034458

10 9 8 7 6 5 4 3 2 1

Published by Sterling Publishing Co., Inc.
387 Park Avenue South, New York, NY 10016
© 2006 by Pep Montserrat
Designed by Randall Heath
Distributed in Canada by Sterling Publishing
c/o Canadian Manda Group, 165 Dufferin Street,
Toronto, Ontario, Canada M6K 3H6
Distributed in the United Kingdom by GMC Distribution Services
Castle Place, 166 High Street, Lewes, East Sussex, England BN7 1XU
Distributed in Australia by Capricorn Link (Australia) Pty. Ltd.
P.O. Box 704, Windsor, NSW 2756, Australia

Printed in China

Sterling ISBN-13: 978-1-4027-3063-4
        ISBN-10: 1-4027-3063-2

For information about custom editions, special sales, premium and corporate purchases, please contact Sterling Special Sales Department at 800-805-5489 or specialsales@sterlingpub.com.

*To my little niece Irene,
please don't stop growing up!*
–PM

MS. RUBINSTEIN'S BEAUTY

by **PEP MONTSERRAT**

Sterling Publishing Co., Inc.
New York

Ms. Rubinstein is a beautiful woman.
But nobody knows it.

Ms. Rubinstein has very beautiful eyes.
But nobody sees them.

Ms. Rubinstein's nose is
wonderful.

But nobody pays attention
to her wonderful nose.

Ms. Rubinstein's pretty hands move harmoniously and delicately.

But nobody notices the delicate harmony of her pretty hands when they move,

or the special grace that her small feet give to the way she walks.

No, nobody notices these things,

because all that people see . . .

. . . is the bushy beard of
Ms. Rubinstein,

MS. Today RUBINSTEIN

the Bearded Lady of Circus Balius, now visiting the city.

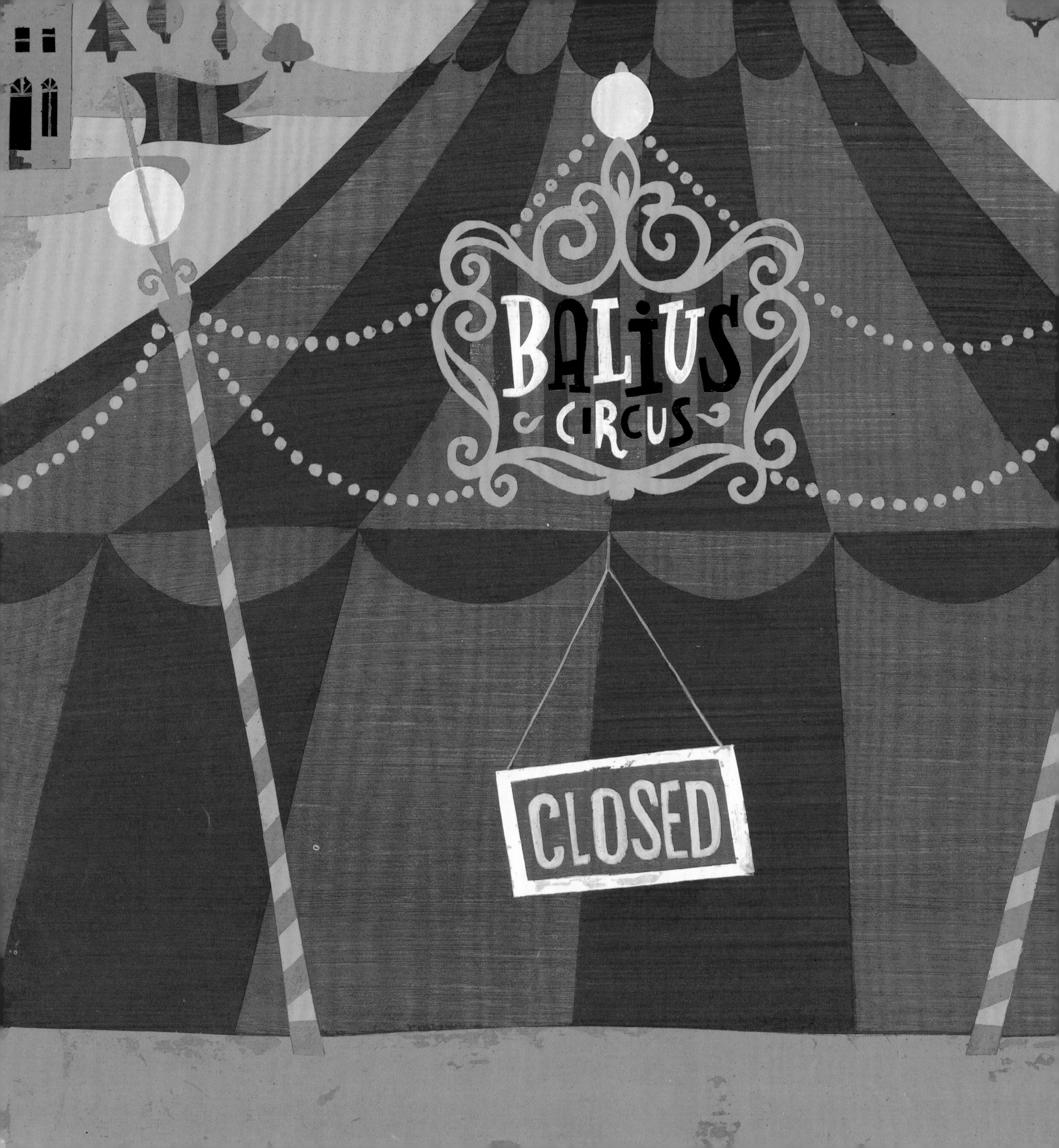
BALIUS
CIRCUS
CLOSED

Today is the circus's day off.
Today there is no show.

That is why Ms. Rubinstein has gone for
a walk to the city park.

She sits on a bench and feeds the pigeons
from a little sack of birdseed that she has
carefully taken out of her handbag.

Everyone in the park at that moment sees only Ms. Rubinstein's bushy beard. No one notices her nice gesture.

No one except the pigeons and
Mr. Pavlov, who now sits next to
Ms. Rubinstein.

Mr. Pavlov secretly notices Ms. Rubinstein's small, graceful feet.

And out of the corner of her eye she sees him sitting and crossing his legs in a very elegant manner.

He discreetly admires the delicate harmony of her hands as she feeds the pigeons, and she, without his noticing, observes his refined way of holding his walking stick.

He admires her wonderful nose while she marvels at the magnificent color of his wavy hair.

Finally, he looks directly
into her eyes . . .

. . . as she meets his.

But their eyes don't see their eyes
anymore, just their hearts.

And their hearts say that they had
been waiting for each other.

And Ms. Rubinstein and Mr. Pavlov
know that this must be . . .

They smile and hold hands in silence as
they take a long walk around the park.

But no one who sees them walking notices
Ms. Rubinstein's beauty.

Or Mr. Pavlov's elegant manner.

Nobody sees their smiles.
Nobody sees the love growing between them.

No, they only have eyes for
Ms. Rubinstein's bushy beard . . .

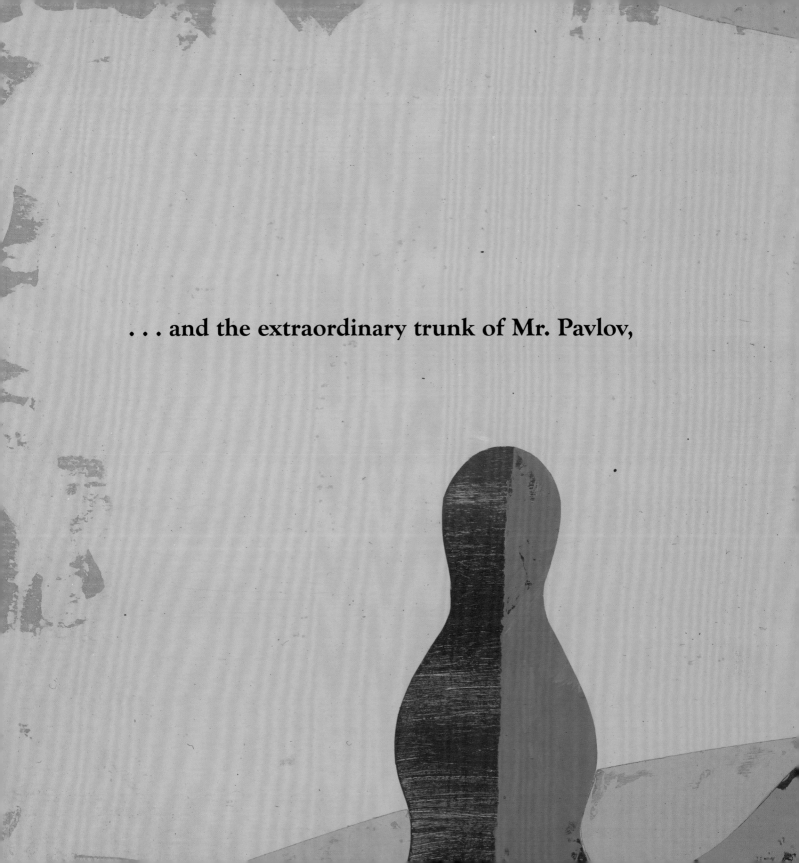

. . . and the extraordinary trunk of Mr. Pavlov,

the Elephant Man
of Circus Guston . . .

. . . also visiting the city.

To all the bearded ladies, including those
who are neither ladies nor bearded.